D1309509

Keep Brushing & Flossing!

all the best,
Heather

Copyright © 2013 Heather Finn

All rights reserved. No part of this book may be
reproduced, transmitted, or stored in an information
retrieval system in any form or by any means,
graphic, electronic, or mechanical, including
photocopying, taping, and recording, without prior
written permission from the publisher.

ISBN: 0988818701
ISBN 13: 9780988818705

Library of Congress Control Number: 2013950549
Little Harbor Books

Visit us at http://littleharborbooks.com

For Matthew, Farrah & Ryan
- My true love bugs
Always,
H.F.

"If you do not brush your teeth they will not grow to be strong and, before you know it, the sugar bugs will come along!"

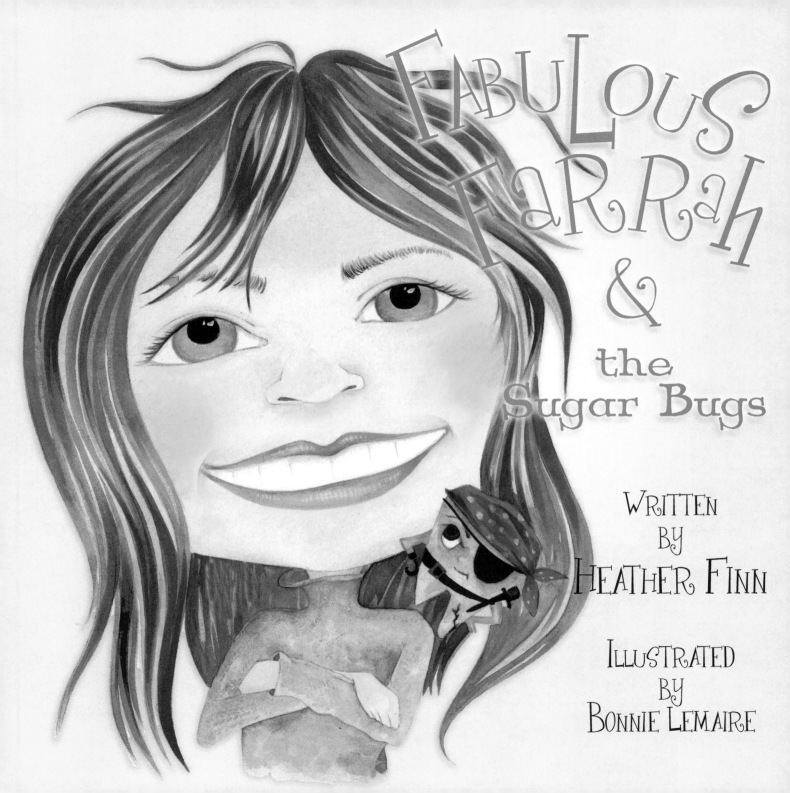

FABULOUS FARRAH

& the Sugar Bugs

WRITTEN
BY
HEATHER FINN

ILLUSTRATED
BY
BONNIE LEMAIRE

I am the fabulous Farrah Feeth! I am eight years old, and I am fabulous at everything I do. Well, *almost* everything.

I can climb a tree like a monkey, my ballet teacher says my *jeté* is absolutely classical, and I have my very own recipe for double-fudge brownies that are perfectly gooey.

FINISH

FINISH

I like to play sports, I hold my school's record for the fastest time in the mile run, and I am told that I have the world's most fabulous smile.

But...to be perfectly honest, there is something you should know about me. I mean, I really cannot even believe I am going to say this out loud, but here goes: I have NOT always had a fabulous smile!

However, I do have a fabulous story about how I got my fabulous smile.

One day I was doing what I considered to be a fabulous job brushing my teeth. But when my mom inspected them, she said, "Hmm. Don't you want to brush until they're nice and bright?"

"Mom, you know that I don't like to brush my teeth," I said. "I have told you many times that it is boring. It takes too long, and I would rather be climbing a tree or making some double-fudge brownies."

My mom smiled. "Honey, I understand what you're saying, but if you aren't careful about brushing your teeth every day, then the Sugar Bugs will find you."

"Mom, *what* are you talking about and *what* is a Sugar Bug?" I asked.

"The Sugar Bugs are a simple way of describing something called *plaque*," mom said. "If you don't brush your teeth really well, and floss too, the sugar and starch from your food and drinks will stick to your teeth and make plaque. Plaque is sticky and slimy, and it's made up of germs and bacteria that eat away at your teeth and give you cavities! Do you want to become known as the not-so-fabulous Farrah Feeth, the girl with the Sugar Bugs all over her teeth?"

"Mom, are you serious?" I said. "If these Sugar Bugs actually do exist, I'm quite sure they would never attack someone as fabulous as me!"

"Fine," said mom. "I'll stop reminding you to brush your teeth. Do you want a snack? How about some potato chips and fruit juice?"

"Yummy!" I said.

For three whole weeks, mom let me eat a lot of sugary and starchy foods like crackers, chips, soda, and juice. I even got to make a batch of my perfectly gooey double-fudge brownies anytime I wanted to, and eat them until I was stuffed.

And mom didn't remind me to brush my teeth even once! So, of course, I kind of forgot to.

Then it was picture day at school. As I was getting ready in the mirror a class mom held up for me, applying some of my fabulous lip gloss, I noticed that my teeth were not pearly white, but a very gross yellowish-green. At that moment I began to panic, because did I happen to mention that it was PICTURE DAY?

Oh, my gosh, I thought, when was the last time I brushed my teeth? I really couldn't remember. All I could think about were the Sugar Bugs and that they were visible for the ENTIRE world to see.

That's when I saw him—and, even worse, he was talking to me!

"I am a Sugar Bug, also known as plaque. I like to attack the sugar on your teeth. I've heard your mom warn you about me, and believe her when she tells you I can be nasty. If I stay on your teeth for too long, they won't grow to be very strong, and without good care, what you'll see is a yucky, mucky cavity."

"Seriously?" I said. "YUCK!"

"Seriously," he said right back to me. "If you don't brush your teeth every day, I will drill little holes in your teeth, and I will give you gum disease and stinky breath, and honestly, nothing makes me happier than stinky breath!"

I didn't know what to do. My class was the first group scheduled for our pictures, and as I was standing in front of the mirror, the class mom handed me a brand-new plastic comb.

"It's time to have your picture taken, Farrah," she said.

All I could think about were the Sugar Bugs crawling all over my teeth. When the photographer said, "Smile," I clamped my mouth shut and gave a closed-mouth smile for the camera.

"Honey, don't you want to give a big smile for the camera?" the photographer said. But I kept my mouth closed and just shook my head from side to side and mumbled, "Nuhuh."

"Come on, Farrah!" the class mom said. "Please show us a smile." But I wouldn't smile for fear that everyone would see my horrible teeth. Even when I was in math, which is my very favorite subject, I answered the teacher's question through closed lips.

"Farrah, what is six times six?" my teacher asked.

That's an easy one, I thought, and replied, "Irdy-ix."

"What did you say?" my teacher said. "I can't quite understand you."

"Irdy-ix," I replied. "Ix imes ix is irdy-ix!"

6 × 6

"Farrah, we cannot understand you," my teacher said. "Please open your mouth and answer the question."

"I an't," I said. "My eeth are irty and I on't ant anyone to ee em."

"Oh, I see," my teacher said. "Your teeth are dirty and you don't want anyone to see them?"

At that point all the kids in the classroom turned and stared directly at me. My face was a bright shade of red and I couldn't even speak. Surely everyone at school would be talking about me and my Sugar Bugs!

But just then the bell rang. Not only did I run all the way home, but I also raced to my bathroom and brushed my teeth until they were shiny and pearly white once again.

Later that night I told my mom about how the Sugar Bugs almost got my teeth.

"I'm going to scrub them away every single day," I said. "And when I brush my teeth, I'll open my mouth wide and use toothpaste with fluoride, and then I'm going to floss between each tooth every day and be a cavity super sleuth."

Mom hugged me. "I know you'll be a fabulous cavity super sleuth."

"Of course!" I exclaimed.

So I started brushing and flossing, and I even took a little travel toothbrush and toothpaste to school with me so I could brush there.

And then one day I was in ballet class and I was supposed to *jeté* in one direction, but I accidentally did a *jeté* the other way and knocked into the girl next to me, who then knocked into the girl next to her, and we all fell on the floor in a tangle of tights and tutus.

The teacher came running up to us, looking mad. I smiled up at her and said, "Sorry."

And she said, "How can I be mad when you have such a fabulous smile, Farrah?" And we all picked ourselves up, brushed ourselves off, and laughed until our bellies hurt.

And that's how I, the fabulous Farrah Feeth, got my fabulous smile!

25679580R00025

Made in the USA
Charleston, SC
12 January 2014